MICHAEL HARDCASTLE

Roar to Victory

Illustrated by Patrice Aitken

The one thing Lee Parnaby wants most in the world is to win the Skalbrooke School-boy Motorcycle Club Intermediates' race. Lee has ambition, determination and courage – all qualities essential for the tough, exciting sport of motor-bike racing. But he's had some set-backs. First there was the race when he fell off his bike. That got Lee an injured shoulder. Then there was serious trouble at the Autodrome track just before he was due to race again. What Lee needs now is luck – and plenty of it!

MICHAEL HARDCASTLE

Roar to Victory

A Magnet Book

Also by Michael Hardcastle in Magnet Books:

IN THE NET
UNITED!
AWAY FROM HOME
FREE KICK
SOCCER SPECIAL
HALF A TEAM
THE TEAM THAT WOULDN'T GIVE IN
THE SATURDAY HORSE
THE SWITCH HORSE
FAST FROM THE GATE
TIGER OF THE TRACK
CAUGHT OUT

First pubished in Great Britain 1982
by Methuen Children's Books Ltd
Magnet paperback edition first published 1983
by Methuen Children's Books Ltd
11 New Fetter Lane, London EC4P 4EE
Reprinted 1983, 1984 (twice) and 1987
Text copyright © 1982 Michael Hardcastle
Illustrations copyright © 1982 Methuen Children's Books Ltd
Printed and bound in Great Britain by
Hazell Watson & Viney Limited,
Member of the BPCC Group,
Aylesbury, Bucks

ISBN 0 416 30070 7

Dedicated, with love, to Barbara, who happily shared the adventures of scrambling

One

On the starting line Lee Parnaby tensed. He tried to crane forward over the handle-bars in the hope of spotting some significant movement on the part of the starter. A good start, a *flying* start, might make all the difference to his chances of success this time. But he had been drawn on the outside of the line of riders and he wasn't able to catch even a glimpse of the man who, at any second, would release the elastic tape.

Just above the heads of the twenty-two moto-cross riders a string of brightly coloured pennants fluttered fiercely in the disturbed air currents. Between the pennants hung numbered discs, each bearing the draw position of the rider stationed beneath it. Japanese and Italian engines quivered and behind the bikes clouds of blue exhaust fumes mushroomed and thickened. At their chosen and strategic points around the circuit spectators nervously bit their lips or offered up prayers or crossed fingers. Among them were parents or close relatives of most of the riders.

Lee hoped, most of all, that there wouldn't be a false start. Once, he himself had caused one, snapping the barrier as his bike seemed to take control of him. Then, when the riders had been recalled by the red flag and the race started properly, Lee's bike had unaccountably stalled and left him stranded. He remembered that as the most humiliating moment of his life.

Now, the tape catapulted sideways and the line instantly broke up as the riders surged forward. No recall flag was waving. The race had begun.

There had been a lot of rain early that morning and there were a few very soft patches of ground on the track. Lee had found one of them in an earlier race and slithered through it uneasily. Now, as the riders built up speed and approached the first bend, a sharp left-hander, the boy on Lee's left touched the edge of another boggy area. He reacted to the danger almost instantaneously; but, as he edged to his right, his front wheel flicked against Lee's knee.

Although the impact was only light Lee's bike wobbled momentarily; and then, neatly changing gear, he had it under control. His confidence suddenly soared as he accelerated towards the corner. Two other bikes had already collided fairly spectacularly on the far side of the track as the second wave of riders began to bunch.

8

The leaders, however, were clear by several metres and beginning to brake for the vital first bend. Whoever led the field at that point would have a considerable advantage. Glancing up, Lee spotted the yellow-and-black stripes of his brother's helmet. They were always easy to pick out at any stage of a race and Darren enjoyed being referred to as 'the Tiger of the Track'. Nonetheless, Darren's success still didn't match that of Graham Relton, the leader in their age-group. Graham had won both the earlier races that afternoon and clearly had made another fine start with the aim of completing a hat-trick. He and Darren went into that first left-hander with not a tyre's width between them.

Lee judged the moment well to change gear again and bump across the deepest of the ruts to avoid being crowded out by a pair of riders on his inside; he recognised one of them and knew that he was always a dangerous opponent in a tight squeeze for room. Yet Lee had managed to pull away from him comfortably.

With the field now well clear of that first bend and the leaders streaking towards the section that wended its way through the fringe of a wood, parents and the keenest supporters were dashing across the track. Most of them had been posted at, or just ahead of, the starting line in order to render immediate assistance if required. However, as

9

soon as their own riders were racing they headed for vantage points from which they could offer maximum vocal encouragement.

'Go on, Jason, get moving, get cracking!' a man in a red jacket was yelling as Lee passed by. 'Move, Jason, move! Don't drop back, whatever you do.'

Lee knew Jason quite well. They attended the same school. He knew that Jason would almost certainly never win a motocross in his life. He didn't even like riding a motor-bike. But his father had enough ambition for both of them and plenty to spare. Lee didn't have to look round to be aware that Jason would be gradually losing touch with the rest of the competitors.

Up ahead, Darren and Graham were still locked in deadly combat. As usual, Graham was riding with flair, saving valuable centimetres by knowing precisely which route to take through a corner or across a slope and still maintain top speed. His balance was exceptional, his style smooth and unhurried. He never seemed to encounter unexpected problems. Graham was used to winning but his determination to win again was the equal of anyone's.

Darren, though, was staying with him at present. He was ready to take risks so as not to lose ground. But his hand on the throttle was sometimes unsteady and there was a constant jerkiness about his riding. Too much of the time he was thinking and worrying about what Graham might do next. He was fearful that Graham would suddenly dash so far ahead he couldn't be caught.

Greatly encouraged by his own good start, Lee settled down to some determined driving. This time he was going to move up on the leaders and remain with them. His greatest wish at the moment was to overtake Darren, to overtake him with a flourish so that Darren would know *at once* who'd passed him; he wanted everyone on the circuit to see that he, the younger brother, had gone ahead. Lee had vowed to himself that one day it would happen, and it might as well be today.

On the narrowest part of the track through the wood he had his first scare of the race. The rider in front of him just clipped one of the bales of straw piled against a tree trunk; the straw was intended to protect competitors but this particular bale was rather too solidly constructed. The Yamaha-mounted rider bounced back from the hay and, in his surprise, lost control of his machine. Suddenly it was sliding sideways across the track and directly in Lee's path.

Automatically, Lee braked – and turned his front wheel to go past the helpless rider on the left. There wasn't much of a gap to go through because by now the stricken motor-bike was practically broadside on to the oncoming riders. Yet, really quite neatly,

Lee managed to squeeze through, touching the offending bale of straw as he did so.

Already a marshal, stationed at that point for just such an occurrence, was leaping on to the track to wrestle with the sprawling Yamaha and get the rider back into the race.

'Well done, son,' he shouted to Lee. 'You're through! Keep going.'

A St John Ambulance man gave him a wave, too, and Lee's spirits were lifting again. He'd been on the edge of trouble but, by his own efforts, he had managed to avoid it.

All the same, he had lost ground on the leaders, as he noted when emerging from the wooded stretch. The circuit came back on itself at that point after describing a couple of 180-degree turns and thus Lee and those in his group appeared to be riding alongside the front runners; in fact, of course, they were on parallel lines.

By now Graham had pulled about a length ahead of Darren and the pair of them were almost a hundred metres ahead of the next rider. Some of the spectators were concluding that it was a two-bike race; and it sounded as though the majority were cheering Graham on to his hat-trick. Such favouritism, however, would merely act as another spur to Darren. But his expression was completely hidden behind his coloured visor. On the straight stretches, however, he was standing higher than

13

usual so that the front wheel was doing no more than skip over the bumps. He himself believed he'd never ridden better.

On the first of the acute hairpins Lee cleverly used his leg for maximum guidance and in doing so he slipped past another rival. So far as he could tell he was now in sixth place, the best position he'd achieved in any race. He was feeling really good. Even the terrifying bomb-hole should be no great obstacle when he was riding like this, he told himself. He thought that was true. Well, perhaps very nearly true.

His bike was running well, too. In the past, he'd had trouble with the timing and he was sure that had cost him dear in some races. That was impossible to prove but it was what he felt. Uncle Ken, who did most of the mechanical servicing of the bike, had been rather dismissive about the trouble. But then, as Lee pointed out, it wasn't his uncle who rode in motocross.

Lee was rapidly approaching the second hairpin. Instinctively, he was in the act of changing down when another rider challenged on his inside. Lee hesitated – and then, to fight off his challenger, he accelerated. Almost immediately, he realised he would have to brake hard in order to negotiate the corner. His foot was late in coming down as a steering aid; and then the back wheel began to slide.

For a split second, he feared that everything was

out of control. He was barely aware of being over-taken by the boy who'd been challenging him. The first Lee saw of him was his back view as the erst-while rival pulled away with noteworthy efficiency. Nervously, Lee regained authority over his own machine and tried to regain his composure.

Quickly, he built up speed again. Yet he was furious with himself for reacting so amateurishly to the sudden presence of the boy who'd been cutting past him. The advantage at such a fierce bend had been with Lee himself because by steering a better course he could have blocked the challenge easily. Instead, he'd momentarily panicked and allowed the other boy to sweep past. He was forced to admit to himself that Darren would never have acted in that way.

There'd been a lot of movement by spectators, crossing from one viewing point to another as the race developed, but the majority of onlookers were perched on the rim of the famous bomb-hole. It really had been made by a bomb – one dropped by a German aircraft in the Second World War. For almost twenty-five years it had lain undetected be-neath the floor of a derelict factory. Then, when it came to light, the Army were called in to explode it under controlled conditions in a wide-open space. The piece of land chosen for the operation was the one now used by the Skalbrooke Schoolboy Motorcycle Club.

Lee felt he was going extremely well along the stretch that launched the riders into the heart-stopping depths of the crater. Once again, he was apparently beginning to overhaul the front runners, all of whom had now emerged from the bomb-hole. There was scattered applause as some boy cleverly skirted trouble on one of the steep slopes; and still louder cheers when he zoomed past another rider in mid air as they took the jump out of the crater together.

The pressure to do well was now at its most intense. Those competitors who hadn't fared too well in the day's earlier races were now absolutely determined to finish with a high position in order to have a chance of picking up a trophy. The awards were made only to the riders who filled the first ten places on the overall performances for the day. Graham Relton and Darren Parnaby were virtually guaranteed to pick up prizes but the battle was still on among the rest of the field for the vital points which would qualify them for a place in the order of merit.

'Go on, go *on*!' an irate father was screeching at a boy on a Suzuki which was slowing down just in front of Lee. For a moment, Lee thought the man was yelling at him. But then, as he swept past the struggling rider, he saw out of the corner of his eye that the Suzuki seemed to be troubled by wheel wobble. Lee even had time to wonder how the man could expect his boy to keep going when he had that sort of dire problem.

The ride was becoming exhilarating to Lee as he continued to make progress through the field. He barely hesitated, mentally or physically, as he reached the edge of the dreaded bomb-hole. At that point he was on his own: every other rider was either beyond the crater or well behind him.

It seemed to Lee that he just flew down the one-in-four gradient. He experienced a glow of excitement and achievement that touched almost every part of his body. With rare nonchalance he swerved round a log that somehow had tumbled into the bottom of the crater; and this time the cheers of the spectators were for him alone. Quite effortlessly, as he thought of it later, he roared up the far slope and then took off from the rim. He landed perfectly with the back wheel thrusting him powerfully forward again.

He had overcome his greatest fear; and now it hardly seemed to have been a fear at all.

The first circuit he completed in what was for him a record time. Once again he had the leaders in sight as he snaked into the wooded section. His concentration now was on overhauling Darren – and even, perhaps, Graham.

Lee saw the yellow flag far too late. It didn't register with his brain quickly enough that there was danger on that fierce S-bend through the trees.

The marshal was holding the flag rather than waving it because he was watching the ambulanceman attend to the rider still sprawled across the track.

Lee powered round the first curve and then, as he straightened up, saw the twin obstacles of fallen rider and horizontal bike.

He knew instantly that he could avoid only one of them.

Two

In spite of making a strenuous effort to miss the two obstructions by steering a path between them Lee cannoned into the front wheel of the fallen bike. Although everything happened very fast it registered with him that it was a Suzuki and that the unavoidable front wheel was still spinning. His own machine stopped dead on impact – and Lee was catapulted over the handle-bars.

The force with which he came down to earth knocked the breath out of his body. Although his first instinct was to get to his feet he found that he couldn't manage that for the moment. He simply gasped for air. Only when he was breathing again did he think about the damage he might have done to himself and his beloved bike.

The ambulanceman temporarily abandoned the unseated rider who'd caused the trouble in the first place and darted across to examine Lee. He'd noted the angle at which Lee had come down and his first fear was that a shoulder had been dislocated. That sort of injury happened all too often to riders who were flung headlong from bikes which stopped abruptly.

His experienced, exploring fingers discovered no obvious disaster. Perhaps, he thought, the lad would be lucky enough to get away with just a few bruises and a shaking-up.

'How do you feel, son?' he inquired gently as Lee's eyes opened for the second time – and this time remained open.

'Er, I'm all right, I think,' was the tentative answer. Lee didn't like to admit to anything he wasn't sure of; but, equally, he hated to appear soft. In any case, his prime concern was the machine he'd been riding.

'Can you get up, then? You'll feel a lot better when you're on your feet,' the ambulanceman continued in a comforting vein. 'You're also still a bit in the way and the last thing we want is for you to get hit again.'

With the man's help, and then an arm round his shoulders, Lee stood up and moved away from the scene of the disaster. The marshal who'd been holding aloft the yellow flag had reacted smartly and wheeled Lee's bike off the track, while one of his companions dealt with the fallen Suzuki and its rider. Meanwhile, the race, of course, was going on as if nothing had happened and the leading machines zipped between the trees. By now Graham had pulled well ahead and there didn't seem to be much that Darren could do to make up the lost ground.

Lee stared in dismay at his motor-cycle. The green-and-silver paintwork no longer gleamed. The machine was smeared with mud and the exhaust appeared to be choked solid with the stuff; so no wonder the engine had cut out.

'How do you feel now, son?' the ambulanceman persisted as he watched the boy's reactions.

'Oh, well, my – er – my shoulder aches a bit – nothing bad, though,' confessed Lee, guessing that it might be best to admit to some minor ailment.

'Ah, well, it would do, wouldn't it, seeing as how you came down on it,' the man said with evident satisfaction. 'So you'll have to take things easy, now, son, and forget this race. Anyway, the leaders are already on the last lap. Nobody's going to catch *them*.'

Lee, vainly trying to remove all the sticking mud, just nodded. He'd known the moment he came off that the race was over for him. His luck was flat out again. What made it so awful this time, though, was that until the crash he'd been riding so masterfully.

'Better get hold of a friend to help you get the old bike back to the paddock,' the first-aid man was suggesting. 'With that dicky shoulder of yours you don't want to go lifting anything heavy.'

'There isn't anyone,' said Lee, without really

21

thinking of what he was saying. He was worrying about possible damage to the engine and the electrical system. The handlebars had taken the brunt of the fall.

'Oh, sorry, son!' The man looked embarrassed and anxious at the same time. 'But you're not on your *own*, are you? I mean, you must have *somebody* with you – if only to transport the old bike to and from the track.'

'There's Uncle Ken. But he'll be waiting for Darren to finish his race. Darren's my brother.'

'Oh, that's good! I mean, I'm glad somebody's looking after you, er – what did you say your name was, son? Lee. Ah, yes. Well, Lee, perhaps we should go and find this Uncle Ken now. Explain that you're all right. He's *bound* to be worried because he hasn't seen you come round the circuit again.'

'I don't suppose he'll really have noticed,' said Lee quietly.

The ambulanceman affected not to hear that comment. He had a word with one of the marshals and explained that he was going to accompany Lee, and his bike, to the paddock now that the Intermediates' race was practically over; he didn't think Lee ought to ride again that afternoon after the shaking he'd received.

Lee was aware of several rather scornful looks from spectators, both adults and boys of his own age, as they made their way to the paddock area which was close to the big public car park. Even if he couldn't ride it, he'd have preferred to push the bike himself but the ambulanceman wouldn't hear of it; so Lee, who sensed that he'd not win an argument, trailed silently along behind him. His shoulder ached a bit but he wasn't going to rub it.

'That's Uncle Ken over there, with my brother,' said Lee quickly as he caught sight of them. 'So I'll take the bike now, thanks, I'll be O.K.'

'Oh,' said the ambulanceman, his eyes opening wider. Lee knew exactly what was coming next; he'd heard it all too often in his life. 'You're twins, then? That must be –'

'No, we're not,' Lee replied, without any expression in his voice. 'He's one year and one day older than I am. So we're not even *nearly* twins. Actually, we're quite different in lots of ways.'

'Oh, well, your brother must be a bit small for his age,' remarked the ambulanceman softly. He had taken a liking to Lee and he hoped he hadn't upset him by mistaking the brothers for twins. 'Right, then, son, I'll leave you in your uncle's good hands. But if your shoulder gives you any real trouble get off to your doctor as fast as you can. Don't want to be laid up for the next Club meeting, do you?'

As he turned away he gave Lee a pat on his undamaged shoulder; and, at that moment, Ken

23

Wragby, who'd been deep in conversation with Darren, glanced up and saw them.

'Hello, Lee, what happened to you, then?' he inquired brightly.

'A bike got in my way,' said Lee as nonchalantly as possible.

'Oh, yeah, I've heard that one before!' Uncle Ken responded with a loud laugh. 'Same thing happened to Darren – a bike ridden by a lad called Graham. A bit useful in the old saddle, is Graham. But Darren's going to get his revenge next time, aren't you, Champ?'

Darren looked only marginally embarrassed at that declaration but he made no reply. Mr Wragby was devotedly examining Darren's new Yamaha. It seemed to Lee that so far his uncle hadn't given even half a glance at Lee's machine. Still, that gave him an opportunity to scrape some of the mud off the swingarm and the exhaust system.

For a few minutes Darren and Uncle Ken discussed the gears of the Yamaha (as far as Lee could tell, Darren was alleging some malfunction as he tried to change 'real fast' into higher gear). Gingerly, Lee tested his left shoulder muscles and found that they protested as he did so. He thought, though, that he should keep exercising them to prevent them from stiffening up. Perhaps it would be a good idea to have a hot bath that night – a decision that would impress his mother, if nothing

else. He just hoped that Darren didn't have the same idea; Lee resented having to share a bath, on top of everything else, with his elder brother.

'Right then, I think I know how to sort that little problem out,' Uncle Ken announced confidently. 'So let's pack up and get off home. No point in staying on to watch the last two races.'

It was he who took charge of Darren's bike while Lee wheeled his own machine to the car park in their wake. Thankfully, his shoulder didn't hurt too much. Just as they came up to their van they passed Graham Relton who was strolling by in the opposite direction.

25

'Congrats on your win, Graham,' Lee said with a grin. On his part, it was an automatic reaction.

'Oh, er, thanks,' Graham muttered, with a sidelong look at Darren and Uncle Ken.

'Thanks *very much*, Lee,' Darren said fiercely as soon as Graham was out of earshot. 'It's nice to know that your own brother is *glad* you lost! True family spirit, that is.'

'Don't be daft,' Lee responded quietly. 'I was just being polite. Graham's a nice guy.'

'So *nice* he tried to knock me off at Victor's Corner, that's all!' Darren raged. 'Shoved me off with his foot as I tried to cut inside. But, naturally, there wasn't a marshal there to see it. Anyway, they're all on Graham's side. Sure is the blue-eyed boy round here.'

'I've never seen him rough-ride anybody,' Lee pointed out. 'Sounds like an excuse to me.'

'Cut out the squabbling, you two!' Uncle Ken ordered as he heaved Darren's bike into the back of the old delivery van. Then, as he took hold of Lee's machine he added, 'You've let this get a bit mucky, haven't you? Get as much of that mud off as you can before we get home, Lee.'

'Sorry,' Lee murmured. He didn't feel apologetic, though. His uncle still hadn't bothered to ask what had happened to him in the race.

While Darren sat up front beside the driver Lee squatted awkwardly in the back and tried to remove

26

as much of the mud as possible. The battered old van had served them well but now it was almost too small for them; and, indeed, Uncle Ken had promised that when they moved up to the Seniors at fourteen, and acquired more powerful bikes, he'd get a bigger vehicle.

Long before they reached his uncle's house in a village on the far side of Skalbrooke Lee was feeling thoroughly fed-up and tired. His arms had been aching even before he started on the cleaning operation. He made a firm promise to himself that he would step up his campaign to improve his stamina and overall fitness. To succeed in the tough and very competitive game of motocross a rider had to maintain peak fitness. Uncle Ken was always stressing that. Darren tended to scoff at that because he thought brains and riding skills were all that really counted; naturally, he believed he possessed both to a high degree. So he didn't bother with any of the muscle-building exercises and weight-training that Lee favoured. Quite regularly he told Lee he was crackers to go in for that stuff, and Lee said nothing in reply because he was accustomed to criticism from his elder brother.

Now, having removed the worst of the mud, he leaned back against the side of the van and listened to Uncle Ken and Darren plotting the downfall of Graham Relton at the next meeting of the Skalbrooke SMC. From the way Darren was talking it was plain that he didn't foresee any difficulty in getting in front, and *staying* in front, when he met his chief rival again. Lee rolled his eyes upwards when he heard that. It was a familiar story; Darren was always *promising* to do this or that – but somehow, when it came to the appointed day, he never quite succeeded in his intentions. But, *of course*, there was invariably a perfect excuse for his failure. Usually Darren had been the victim of another rider's cunning cheating . . . or he'd been terribly unlucky to suffer a mechanical failure . . . or a rival had collided with him accidentally and put him out of the race. Darren, according to Darren, never made simple mistakes himself. Things that went wrong were definitely somebody else's fault.

'You're very quiet, Lee,' said his uncle, swinging round to glance at him.

'Oh, er, yes,' Lee, startled, agreed. There hadn't been much opportunity to be anything else with Darren chatting away non-stop. 'I was, er, just thinking.'

'Thinking about food, I imagine. Well, I expect your aunt will have something good for us as usual. Won't be long now.'

Lee would have laughed if he'd felt in better spirits. For some reason he'd never been able to understand, his uncle had the idea that Lee was forever starving and therefore needed to be supplied with food in great quantities as often as possible. It was a complete fallacy. Lee's appetite was just normal and scarcely any bigger than Darren's. Yet their uncle wasn't constantly trying to force food down Darren's throat. Fortunately, Aunt Sue treated the matter as a bit of a joke and would say that Lee wasn't as skinny as that. Nonetheless, she always gave him a good portion of everthing and seemed pleased when he ate up.

While his uncle and Darren fussed about with the bikes in the workshop behind the house on arriving home, Lee went into the kitchen to get a drink of orange juice or anything else that would quench his sudden thirst. Sometimes they all had a meal almost immediately they returned from a meeting. On those occasions Uncle Ken took his nephews to their own home fairly early in the evening. He worked as a regional sales manager for a company that made canned foods, and occasionally he had to set off on a Sunday evening to be in time for a sales conference the following day.

'Ah, hello, Lee,' Aunt Sue greeted him cheerfully as she breezed into the kitchen. 'Had a good day? Pick up a trophy?'

'Er, no, not exactly. Actually, I came off and didn't even finish the race. My shoulder aches a bit but there's nothing wrong with it, really.'

Mrs Wragby gave him a calculating look. 'Um, well, you do look *a bit* grim – and a bit muddy, too.

Listen, why don't you treat yourself to a nice hot bath and soak any old aches and pains away? There's plenty of hot water and the meal won't be ready for at least an hour.'

'Oh, great! Yes, I'd really like that.'

She was both surprised and amused by his rapid acceptance of the offer. As he turned towards the stairs, she added, 'Oh, Lee, have you had any news this week from your Dad?'

'No.' That was his instant reaction. Then, relenting slightly, he said, 'Well, Mum had a postcard from Panama. Nothing for Darren or me – as usual.'

'Oh, well,' said Aunt Sue brightly. 'Perhaps his next leave will be a really long one and then he can spend lots of time with you. Now, then, I suppose I'd better go and have a word with those other motor-cycle maniacs and see what they're up to. Enjoy your bath, Lee.'

As he reclined in the luxuriously warm water and enjoyed the solitude, Lee found his thoughts drifting to his father, who was in the Merchant Navy, and wondering where his ship might be now. His communication with his family when he was away for months on end was infrequent, to say the least, but sometimes spectacular: he would telephone from the middle of an ocean in the middle of an English night. When that happened their mother would arouse Lee and his brother to have a few words with him, words all too often splintered by atmospherics or lack of concentration because the boys were still half asleep.

Yet, when he was at home, Brian Parnaby took remarkably little interest in the activities of his sons. It was his brother-in-law, Ken Wragby, who inspired and involved himself in their enthusiasms.

'Lee! Lee, are you awake in there?' a voice was calling; and a hand was slapping against the bathroom door. It was a moment before Lee realised who it was: Joanne, his cousin, almost a year younger than himself. 'Listen, Mum's sent you a mug of coffee. I've brought it for you. Shall I bring it in?'

'Er, no, no, thanks, Jo!' He sat up and shot an anxious glance at the door; and saw, to his relief, that he had remembered to lock it. 'The door's locked. Leave it outside, would you?'

She laughed. 'Oh, I was going to! 'Bye, then.'

He waited a minute or so and then went to retrieve the coffee. Then, just as he was taking the first sip, someone else banged heartily on the door.

'Hey, come on out of there,' yelled Darren. 'I want to use the bathroom.'

Lee looked at the locked door with immense satisfaction.

'Well, hard lines, Daz,' he called. 'This time, you'll just have to wait for me, won't you?'

Three

It had not been a good day, in any way, for Lee. As, painstakingly, he completed a larger-than-life-size drawing of the human eye, his mind wandered over the events of the past few hours. His first mistake of the day had been to smash a teapot, his second to turn his back on a cricket ball that must have been travelling at about a hundred miles an hour. In addition to those mishaps, he'd somehow managed to upset quite a number of people.

For some reason, he'd overslept that morning, perhaps because he'd had a restless night with disturbing dreams. His mother, supposing wrongly that Darren had awakened him because they slept in the same room and Darren was already downstairs, hadn't come upstairs to tell him what time it was and to hurry up. She, it turned out, had also had a poor night and so wasn't in the best of moods. Then, when he did belatedly come down for his breakfast, he'd been in such a rush he'd knocked the china teapot flying with the swirling tail of his jacket. Uncompromisingly, his mother had insisted that he clean up the mess before going off to school, though Lee pointed out that he was going to miss his bus.

'You've missed your usual bus, so another one missed isn't going to make any difference,' she replied.

'Oh, Mum, that's not fair!' he protested.

'*Life's* not fair,' was her final comment.

That was already Lee's verdict and it was confirmed as soon as he arrived at school and collected two penalty points for being half-an-hour late – and then ran foul of the sports master who was taking Lee's class for cricket coaching.

Cricket wasn't a game that he cared for and Mr Burns guessed as much. So, when Lee dropped a relatively easy catch, he was ordered to field closer to the bat at the suicidal position of forward short leg. 'If you're nearer to the ball when it leaves the bat you might stand a chance of holding on to it,' snorted Mr Burns, who insisted on everyone taking every game and training session seriously. Unfortunately, the bowler dropped the ball short, the batsman swung powerfully, connected crisply – and Lee tried to get out of the way of the bullet-like shot. Luckily for him it was the fleshy part of the leg that took the impact but it was an exceedingly

33

painful blow. Lee had hopped about frantically but Mr Burns was unsympathetic.

'I don't expect you put on a performance like that when you fall off your motor-bike, Lee, so there's no need for that sort of carry-on,' he said sharply.

Several of the class had a good laugh at that; but they were the ones, of course, who were deeply envious of Lee's opportunities to compete in moto-cross events.

Even now, as the school day was dragging to a close, Lee could still feel the effects of that crack on the back of his thigh. There could be no doubt that

34

he would have a multi-coloured bruise by now. Of
course, it was hardly in a place where he could
examine its development at present. Still, he managed a grin at the thought of how he'd got out of
the firing line as a result of his injury: the sports
master had sent him to assist the groundsman to
roll the pitch. As luck had it, the groundsman was
a superbike fanatic and so they'd had a good chat
about the merits of various motor-cycles.

'Ah, you find the aqueous humour a subject for
some amusement of your own, do you, young Parnaby?' Mr Curzon, the biology teacher, asked with
sudden, and heavy, sarcasm. It was the sort of

witticism that some members of the class would appreciate, he knew, and he smirked at the dutiful laughs.

'Er, no, sir,' Lee replied carefully. He'd just labelled that part of the eye between the cornea and the lens and so he knew that aqueous humour was a fluid, nearly pure water, contained in that space. It was typical of Swearer, as everyone called Mr Curzon beyond his hearing, to pick on that word for his joke. 'I think my face must have, er, slipped.'

'Quite!' the biology teacher shot back instantaneously. 'You and I have never seen eye to eye, Lee!'

Once again his remark triggered off a volley of more laughs and even cheers. It seemed to Lee that Swearer was trying to win back his popularity with the class. Earlier in the double period he had exploded with rage because some boys had fooled about during an experiment involving the cutting up of a dead animal. The whole class had been punished with a written test so hard that nobody could manage to get more than half the answers right. So the outcome of that was to be another test, later in the week, for which they would have to do extra homework. What was so infuriating to Lee was that he hadn't been even remotely involved in the dissection of the vole; but everyone had to suffer because of the stupidity of one small group.

As soon as Swearer Curzon had turned away to

torment somebody else about the location of the 'blind spot' in the eye – where the optic nerve leaves the retina – Lee took a surreptitious glance at his watch. Only another five minutes to go and then the school day would be over. He had it in mind to go along to the leisure centre and make use of the multi-gym: he was anxious to strengthen the muscles in his arms and legs to help his riding and improve his stamina. Since the last meeting of the Skalbrooke SMC when he'd crashed into the Suzuki almost a fortnight had gone by; but, because of homework and essential jobs he'd had to do around the house there had been few opportunities to do much training.

Piercingly, the final bell rang.

Half the class clattered to their feet immediately, calling to one another or scrambling to be the first to reach the door. None of them managed it. Swearer planted himself in front of the exit and ordered everyone to sit down again. He looked, as someone remarked later, livid. For almost a minute he told them what he thought of them; and for several minutes they sat in complete silence. Even when Swearer did at last let them go they had to file out without a word being spoken.

Lee dashed for the front entrance of the building the split-second he was clear of the classroom. He'd promised to meet Bobbie Keenan and repay him the pound he'd borrowed the previous day. Bobbie was the sort of lad who always had money to spare and so when Lee somehow lost his dinner money Bobbie was the obvious one to approach for a loan. Unfortunately, with over-sleeping and being in such a rush that morning Lee had forgotten to ask his mother for some extra money; and thus, at dinnertime, he'd had to borrow from Darren to repay Bobbie's loan.

'Oh, it's O.K., it didn't really matter today,' Bobbie remarked casually when Lee paid the money over and apologised for being late.

'Oh no,' said Lee earnestly, 'I hate being in debt.'

As, thankfully, he started on his way home at last, Lee thought about the money situation. While it was true that he disliked owing anything he knew that he was sometimes very careless about money. He never worried about it and didn't often even think about it. If he had money, that was fine; if he had none, well, that was just too bad. Darren, on the other hand, always had money, however much he spent, and he knew to the penny how much was in his pocket at any given moment. Even when today's loan to his brother was repaid, Darren would remember for a very long time exactly how much, and for how long, Lee had borrowed from him.

Because he was absorbed by his thoughts Lee didn't immediately notice the scuffle taking place just ahead of him in Boston Grove. It was a narrow, tree-lined thoroughfare that provided a short cut on the way to the bus stop. Its only notable feature was a half-derelict Methodist church, surrounded by tall railings and flanked by an alleyway that led to a row of terraced houses. For anyone wanting to set an ambush it was an ideal spot.

Suddenly Lee became aware that a couple of boys were rushing across the road from the entrance to the church. He recognised one of them as Andy Haylin, a loud-mouthed, beefy character who was going to win every event he entered on sports day – according to him. His father had been a third-class professional wrestler in his time and Haylin was always relating the story of how he'd once won a contest on television.

'Right, then, Parnaby, let's see you scramble up there,' he was yelling. 'That will show how good *you* are!'

Then he grabbed his mate round the shoulders and together they leaned back against the wall facing the church and guffawed.

Lee drew level with the entrance and, glancing down the flagged path, saw his brother standing by the porch. With a forlorn expression, Darren was staring up at the sharply sloping roof. Lying against the tiles at such an angle it might almost have been stuck there by super-glue, was a briefcase. Even without Darren's presence, Lee would have had no difficulty in identifying its owner. The case, in soft calfskin with brass locks, was probably his brother's second most prized possession. Like the first, his motor-cycle, it had been a gift from Uncle Ken.

'Why is it up there?' Lee asked quietly, coming up behind Darren.

His brother swung round, his eyes now flashing angrily as he caught sight of Haylin and his accomplice.

'Because that stupid pair of maniacs are jealous, that's why! They can't win anything off their own bat so they try to bring everyone down to their own rotten level. They heard me talking about scrambling so they chucked the case up there.' He stopped and then added in a whisper, 'Lee, how did they know I can't stand heights?'

'I don't suppose they did. I expect it's just Haylin's way of trying to make things as difficult as possible. Typical of him. Anyway, I'll get it for you – if I can reach it. You know climbing doesn't bother me.'

Lee was sizing up the task as he spoke. The idea of scaling rock faces had always appealed to him when he saw climbers in action on television; but he'd not had an opportunity of finding out whether he was really capable of it. The best he'd achieved was in an old quarry when he'd climbed several metres to retrieve a child's escaped kite: that had been much easier than he'd imagined.

'It's a bit sheer, isn't it?' Darren pointed out uneasily. 'I mean, what can you get a grip on?'

'Well, there's that bit of drainpipe up there, if it hasn't rusted too badly. The bricks aren't in good shape, so they'll be easier to grasp. You watch to see if anything shows signs of breaking up. O.K.?'

'Look, Lee, I think I'd better see if I can borrow a ladder or something. I mean, if anything happens, Mum'll go mad – mad with me. And –'

'Just watch, Daz, just watch. We're not giving Haylin a free load of laughs.'

The easiest part of the whole operation was to get up on to the wide sill of the ground-floor window and Lee didn't even need to ask for any assistance. The glass had disappeared long ago in an outbreak of vandalism and the opening had been boarded up with the sort of efficiency that ensured no one would get in without a lot of hard effort. Lee grasped one of the struts, pulled himself up and then stepped sideways along the sill towards the drainpipe.

'It looks a bit risky to me, Lee,' his brother said worriedly.

Lee just shrugged, which in itself was a slightly hazardous gesture to make. He guessed he looked more confident than he felt but now he'd launched himself into the recovery business he wasn't going to give up without very good cause.

The pipe seemed to be secure. With one hand on

the pipe and the other on the projecting bricks that formed the decorative arch of the window, he quickly gained height. He was very thankful that the shoes he was wearing had rubber soles – and ribbed rubber at that.

From the other side of Boston Grove there came a faint cheer that was intended to be ironic. But it sounded half-hearted. Andy Haylin and his confederate were rapidly concluding that their victim's brother was a pretty determined character. They knew a great deal about their class-mates but hardly anything about the younger boys at the school. So they had no idea what Darren's brother was really like; and they'd made the mistake of assuming he was exactly like Darren.

Lee barely heard them. He was concentrating completely on transferring his weight from the top of the window arch to a secondary drainpipe which forked away from the main pipe at the convenient angle of about 45 degrees. If he could gain a foothold on that he should then be able to make excellent progress towards the roof.

He was just about to swing himself across to the pipe when Haylin yelled as loud as he could manage, 'You'll never make it, kiddo! That pipe won't hold even your skinny weight. You've had it!'

His sole intention was to unnerve Lee and he very nearly succeeded. The climber made the elementary error of trying to glance towards the speaker. His searching right foot missed its toe-hold and next moment was scrabbling desperately across the face of the wall.

Darren's face lost its colour in an instant. He clenched his fingers so tightly the nails bit into the palms.

'Pack it in now, Lee,' he called in anguish. 'I don't care about the case. Just leave it and get down! I mean it.'

Lee's right shoe at last wedged itself against a bracket. He paused and expelled a long breath. The worst was over. He was sure of that. For a moment, he'd thought he was going to fall. Now he felt quite safe again. Lee wouldn't allow himself to be distracted again by anything – or anyone. His determination to reach the briefcase had simply been increased by Haylin's stupid call. He had barely heard Darren's voice.

The rest of the route to the roof presented no problems at all. After testing the guttering and finding it ready to drop off at any moment he edged his way to the far wall and pulled himself on to the tiles from that direction. The angle of the roof was steep enough for him to decide to lie flat against the tiles – and then wriggle his body across to the briefcase. He was calm and confident; he could even think about those watching him and guess that *they* were supposing he was terrified.

Within a minute he had reached his objective.

With his outstretched left hand he grasped the corner of the case and pulled it towards him. Then, taking hold of the handle, he yelled, 'Here it comes, Daz! Don't drop it now.'

With a flick of his wrist he sent the briefcase spinning up over the guttering in a neat arc. Darren moved a couple of paces and then took the case into his arms like a rugby full-back receiving the ball from a high kick.

'Got it!' he called to his brother. 'Well done, Lee.'

Then he turned round to see the reaction of Haylin and his pal. But the ex-wrestler's son and his fellow thug had vanished. Darren could smile again. With Lee's help, he'd defeated them.

'Thanks, kiddo,' he said warmly when Lee reached the ground. He even went so far as to put his arm round his brother's shoulders. 'I'll do something for you when I get the chance.'

'O.K.,' Lee said, shrugging. 'I'll hold you to that one day.'

As they strolled out of Boston Grove, however, Lee was thinking that he didn't care whether Daz repaid the debt. In a way, he hoped it would be forgotten – well, no, not forgotten, exactly, but perhaps ignored until it was necessary to use it as an advantage in some way. The one thing he himself would have to remember was to repay Darren the money he'd borrowed in order to pay Bobbie.

44

Darren, now swinging his briefcase contentedly, didn't keep him company for long. Spotting some of his cronies as they rejoined the main road he simply said, 'See you when we get home, Lee,' and then dashed away. In recent years it had become plain to Lee that Darren couldn't bear to be seen with a younger boy, even if that boy was his brother. Odd, really, but that's how it was, as Lee had pointed out to his own friends who expressed surprise about the relationship.

When, at last, he dropped off the bus close to his home, his thoughts were fixed on his training session that evening at the local leisure centre. Perhaps it was time to alter his routine in the weight-lifting exercises so that he could try to build up –

'Hey, don't I get so much as a grin from you today, young Lee?' a familiar voice interrupted his planning.

'Oh, er, hello, Mr Thirlwell. Sorry I didn't notice you.'

'Nor would you have done if I hadn't spoken up. Deep down you were in some rare old thoughts. Homework is it, that's bothering you?'

Mr Thirlwell was a travelling greengrocer with a van that was said to be older than he was. Darren had once described it, rather contemptuously, as a shoebox on four wheels. Rectangular it certainly was, with just the cab and the snub-nose engine to break up the severe lines, but Mr Thirlwell kept it

in beautiful condition. There never seemed to be a speck of dirt to mar its orange and chocolate-brown paintwork and the brass handles on the doors gleamed with polish. Its owner and Lee had been friends for years, ever since the day, in fact, when Lee, standing beside his mother as she bought vegetables and fruit, announced loudly to the world that the van was 'the smartest and bestest car in the whole world.' His immediate reward had been a ride in the 'bestest' along the entire length of the street, during which journey he had taken alternate bites of the apple and the banana that had also been given to him by the delighted owner-driver.

47

'No, no, homework's no worry,' replied Lee, leaning against the side of his favourite vehicle. 'Haven't got any for tonight. It's my get-fit training I was thinking about – you know, to make me a *stronger* rider. To improve my stamina, really.'

'What you need is vitamins, young Lee. Vitamins – and plenty of 'em. They'll give you all the stamina you need.' Mr Thirlwell was warming to a favourite theme and Lee hastily stopped leaning and prepared to bolt. 'Now, take my lemons and oranges, for instance. Just packed full of Vitamin C, they are, and –'

'Sorry, Mr Thirlwell, I've just got to dash! I'm already late for tea and Mum gets really mad, you see. Oh yes, and my cousin'll be here, so I've got to entertain her, that's what Mum says. . .'

The greengrocer shook his head sadly as Lee, still trying to offer excuses over his shoulder, sped along the avenue. He'd been going to present the lad with a few of his vitamin-packed oranges to boost his suspect stamina.

Four

'I am beginning,' said Mrs Parnaby stonily, 'to despair of you, Lee. You'd turned it into a ruinous day before you left for school this morning – and now it looks as though you're trying to end it on the same note. Well, it's not good enough.'

For a few moments she buttered slices of bread in tight-lipped fury. Lee could only wait apprehensively for the next onslaught. He rather feared that she might decide he wasn't to be allowed any tea at all. If that happened, he didn't think he would survive the rest of the day.

'You could surely see this instructor at the gymnasium on some other evening, couldn't you?' his mother continued relentlessly. 'There *are* other evenings in the week when he could give you the undoubted benefit of his expertise, I'm certain. So –'

'No, he *isn't* there every night, Mum,' Lee cut in. 'It's tonight when he's able to *help* me with the

49

weights in the right ratios. It's all *fixed*, he *told* me what time to be there.'

His first statement was true; the second would not have stood up to a severe examination by anyone who knew all the facts. Lee could only pray that his mother wouldn't spot any flaws.

'Well, if that's the arrangement then you'd better go,' she announced heavily. 'I don't want you to earn a reputation for letting people down. Though you've certainly let Joanne down. So you'd better go straight through and apologise to her. And tell her that tea's almost ready. Go on.'

He went through into the lounge where Joanne was watching television. She visited them once a week, though not always on the same day, for a meal. That was one way, Mrs Parnaby had explained, of repaying the hospitality and generosity of the Wragbys to Darren and Lee.

'Jo, I'm sorry about this, but I've just got to go out tonight,' he told her with what he thought was a convincing display of disappointment. In fact, he really did like his cousin and usually they got on well together. 'So I'm afraid you'll have to, er, amuse yourself.'

'Well, that won't be difficult. I'm used to it,' she replied brightly. 'You always are when you're an only one.'

Lee ran his hand through his helmet of hair that was the colour of honey. 'Yeah, I know how you feel. It's like that here most of the time. I mean, I didn't even *know* Daz was going out to tea tonight at one of his mates. But I get the blame for not looking after you.'

'I expect younger ones are always the ones that suffer,' remarked Joanne with an understanding smile. 'At least I'm spared that! I expect it's something special you are going out to, isn't it, Lee?'

He told her about his plans to build up his stamina so that when he rode in motocross he wouldn't get tired however tough the course and however severe the conditions. As ever, Joanne listened attentively and asked only intelligent questions. Lee knew that she didn't discuss such matters with Darren; his brother had no time for her. Lee thought she knew a great deal about bikes and scrambling. No doubt she picked most of it up from listening to her father, though Uncle Ken normally didn't say much to her when Lee and Darren were there.

'Well, anyway, there's something good on television tonight, so I'll enjoy that instead,' Joanne said reassuringly when Lee's mother raised the matter of his departure for the umpteenth time during the meal.

'That's great, Jo,' he responded gratefully. 'And I'll make it up to you soon – take you somewhere special you'd like to go.'

'You will that,' his mother added firmly.

As he hurried down the avenue after leaving the house Lee couldn't help feeling guilty about the way he'd abandoned Joanne; and he was thankful that she hadn't asked to come and watch him doing his training. It was a wonder his mother hadn't suggested that, but perhaps she considered that a gymnasium was no place for a young girl. Lee suspected, though, that Jo would have enjoyed the experience.

He was waiting impatiently for the bus to arrive when, without warning, a passing vehicle suddenly swerved towards the kerb and then screeched to a

halt a couple of metres from where Lee was standing. The next instant a familiar face was grinning at him through the passenger's window and calling to him to get a move on. Greg Shearsmith, a fellow motocross rider, was forever in a hurry.

'Where you going, then?' Greg demanded to know. Then, when he'd been given an answer, he immediately countered, 'Oh, that's no good, Lee! The only training that's any good is on the bike. Got to ride all the time to be a winner. Right, Dad?'

'Right, son,' confirmed Mr Shearsmith, sitting behind the steering wheel of the Volkswagen minibus. 'So let's get going, O.K.? Give your pal here a lift and talk on the way.'

'Thanks very much,' said Lee, climbing in. It occurred to him that he'd be saving a bus fare besides getting to his destination faster.

'Look, don't bother with that weight-lifting rubbish tonight,' Greg resumed as soon as they were moving. 'I could use a bit of help, so come and do some bike training with me. We're testing my new bike – it's on the trailer. But it's under wraps because we don't want too many people to see what we've done.'

Lee hesitated. The idea was tempting; but, on the other hand, he didn't much care for Greg, an aggressive, almost bullying, type who thought nothing of literally knocking other riders out of his path in scrambles. Occasionally, though, he rode quite brilliantly. His father was known to be well off and, just as usefully, a skilled mechanic.

Greg, who had the shortest haircut of any boy Lee had ever seen, was looking at him with an eagerness for a favourable answer that Lee found surprising.

'Lee, I know you haven't got your own bike now because you keep it at your uncle's, right?' he rushed on. Lee just nodded. 'So, O.K., maybe you can have a go on mine – we'll see how it works out. But Dad's got this meeting he can't get out of so he can't do the timing and that sort of stuff. He'll come and pick us up later and get you home again. You can do your own riding a lot of good by coming with me and training where it matters – on the track, on a *bike*. A real racer, too.'

Lee hastily buried his doubts.

'O.K., then, Greg. It's true, I do miss not having my machine at home. The garden's not big but I could get *a bit* of riding practice. Did you say you had a *new* bike? What is it?'

'A Shearsmith Special!' Greg declared to Lee's astonishment. 'Yeah, honest! Dad's designed it himself and it's great – I absolutely know it's going to be the greatest bike Skalbrooke's ever seen. But it's all secret until I ride it at the next meeting in a fortnight.'

'Well, I'll know a lot about it if you let me try it

54

out tonight,' Lee pointed out. 'So it won't exactly be a secret then, will it?'

'Oh, but I can trust *you*, Lee,' was Greg's reply to that.

Rather to his own surprise, Lee was pleased by that compliment. He began to see Greg Shearsmith in a different light. Perhaps the rest of the club members had been misjudging him and mistaking his enthusiasm for win-at-all-costs aggression. It was certainly both sporting and generous of him to allow another rider – a rival – to train on his new, and obviously very special, machine.

They fell to discussing the previous meeting of the Skalbrooke SMC and it wasn't until Mr Shearsmith brought the Volkswagen to a halt and switched off the engine that Lee realised where they'd been heading.

'We're at the Autodrome!' he exclaimed. 'But we can't practise here, Greg – it's where the next meeting is being held. It's against the rules to ride on a circuit before a meeting.'

'Ah, but we're being cunning, aren't we?' Greg replied with a note of satisfaction in his voice. 'We're not going to go on the track itself, just *alongside* it. Nothing in the rules to say we can't do that. Right, Dad?'

'Right, son,' said Mr Shearsmith, disappearing behind the minibus to unhitch the trailer. Greg followed eagerly, Lee glumly. He felt he ought to

55

ask Mr Shearsmith to take him back into town but, somehow, he thought the man would refuse. If Greg wanted Lee's assistance, Greg would have it. His father would see to that.

With loving care, the new bike was removed from its stand on the trailer; and Lee couldn't help feeling envious when he studied it.

'You like it, then?' inquired Greg, letting his fingers trail tenderly over the gleaming black paint of the fuel tank, and then caress the fabric, equally black, of the saddle. Lee just nodded. Mere words seemed inadequate.

'It's the exhaust system that makes it so special,' Greg continued, stooping to pat the ringed barrel attached to the exhaust pipe. 'I get a wider spread of power, you see. And a bit extra on top speed. Dad's brilliant at tuning and getting a different power delivery.'

'So you'd better match that brilliance with your riding,' said Mr Shearsmith crisply as he nipped back into the minibus. 'Don't do anything daft, Greg. Don't draw attention to yourself. You never know who may be wandering over the Autodrome – courting couples, bird watchers, poachers with shotguns. So be careful. I'll be back as soon as I can. Cheers, then!'

Greg was plainly pleased to see him go, so that he could get on with the business of riding. He waited, though until the Volkswagen was out of

sight before putting on his kit. From helmet, to new leathers with knee protector caps, to smooth-soled boots, he dressed slowly, enjoying the feel and fit of every item. It was quite a theatrical performance and Lee watched in some amusement. Already it had occurred to him that if he was to be given a ride, he would have to borrow some of Greg's kit as, of course, he had none of his own with him.

'I thought your Dad would have wanted to stay to see how you got on,' he observed. 'I mean, he's pretty keen on your riding – and the bike.'

Greg adjusted the body-belt which he wore under his leathers to protect his kidneys in the event of a bad fall. 'I know,' he agreed, 'but this meeting of his is about finance and he's the treasurer, so he didn't have any option. Anyway, he's had a go himself on the Shearsmith Special so he *knows* it's terrific. And, naturally, he knows I'm a terrific rider! So he doesn't need to act like a – like a watchdog.'

The ebony special throbbed into exciting life and Greg bobbed away at a surprisingly sedate speed. Lee watched as his old rival – though now, he supposed, Greg would have to be accepted as a new friend – went round in a wide sweep as if to demonstrate what excellent balance he possessed. The turf was springy and quite dry, for the Autodrome was on the edge of wide moors across which winds were forever sweeping. At one time it had been an Air Force base and remnants of the runways and taxi-ing paths were still used occasionally for motor-racing events, particularly on bank holidays.

The Schoolboy Motor-cycle Club paid a fee to use the place and its facilities on a regular basis, and thus had been permitted to construct their own circuit within the boundaries formed by the runways. Because some excavations had been carried out in one area during a search for ancient remains, one or two hollows had formed and deepened during the years of neglect; and, inevitably, they had been incorporated into the club's circuit. There were no trees but a handful of impenetrable bushes constituted the major hazards so far as vegetation was concerned.

It was a very fast track. Oval in design, it contained two long, undulating straights along which riders of Greg's nature were bound to score on the basis of speed alone. But it also featured a couple of V-turns: and those V's, as someone had remarked, stood for Vicious. The bikes had to be more or less 'walked' round those bends.

'Right, what do you think of the Special, then?' Greg called out as he rode back towards Lee after completing another wide circle, this time in an anti-clockwise direction.

'Looks great,' Lee admitted.

'It *feels* great,' Greg enthused, boosting the

59

engine note to a healthy roar. 'Now I'll show you what we can do together.'

For a moment, Lee supposed Greg was referring to some sort of partnership between them; but then it became clear that he was talking about himself and his bike. From some concealed pocket he produced a stopwatch and handed it over.

'I'm going to do one circuit just to warm up,' he explained. 'Then, second time round I want you to time me. You can station yourself at V-One and put the clock on the moment I come out of that turn. Then later on, when I go again I'll be out to beat my first record. O.K.?'

'Well, all right,' Lee said a trifle doubtfully. 'But I thought you promised me a ride sometime.'

'Oh sure,' Greg replied nonchalantly as he pulled his goggles into place. 'But I've got to set that top time first. Better get yourself off to V-One, Lee, 'cos it won't take me long to get there, you know.'

With a splendid eruption of blue smoke, the Shearsmith Special surged away and in a matter of moments the rider was motoring at full chat. As he turned on to the circuit, Greg hadn't a care in the world.

Frowning, Lee made his way to the acute bend known to every club member as V-One. He couldn't suppress the feeling that Shearsmith was simply intending to employ him as a timekeeper.

As the scintillating Special disappeared from

sight and the engine note faded Lee thought he heard, distantly, the bark of a dog. He scanned the horizon but could see no sign of any animal. Dogs, he was well aware, could be a real problem to motor-cyclists if they took a dislike to bikes for any reason. So far the Autodrome had appeared to be deserted and he was keeping his fingers crossed that it would stay that way.

By now Lee was in the middle of the circuit and he turned to watch Greg flash by on the first of the straights. Greg was confident enough to give him a wave – and at that point he was actually crouching low in the saddle to cut down wind resistance. Lee guessed that the Special could be approaching a speed of 50 m.p.h.; but Greg wouldn't be able to sustain that much longer. Already he was leaning into a curve.

Lee descended into the slight dip where V-One was located. Not for the first time he thought what a fearful turn it was.

One half-minute of blissful peace he had all to himself. In the next half-minute or so, everything seemed to happen.

He looked to his left as he heard the noise of the Special's engine. It seemed to Lee that Greg really ought to be slowing down by now to negotiate the notorious bend in safety. Then, just as Greg began to brake, a small dog hurtled over the low banking and rushed straight at the bike.

Somehow, and it was to his great credit, Greg managed to swerve away from the dog, a short-haired terrier. In doing so, however, he lost control; and, as he fell off, the bike charged up the slope on its own before losing momentum. Greg, momentarily stunned, lay where he had fallen, with the dog snapping at his helmet.

Lee, seeing what would happen next if he didn't prevent it, darted across the track and up the incline. The bike was now slithering back towards Greg, and would have crashed into him and the dog if Lee hadn't grabbed the handle-bars and heaved

with all his strength. To his great relief, he arrested its ominous progress.

Suddenly, two men appeared above the banking – and, as they stared at the scene below, one of them began to call off the dog.

At that moment Greg sat up, pushed back his helmet and yelled, 'You stupid fools! Don't you realise it's murder to let a dog loose on a racing track?'

Lee glanced at the men to see their reaction and froze. He was so astounded he almost dropped the Shearsmith Special.

One of the men was Mr Cantrill, secretary of Skalbrooke SMC and a figure of total authority. He ran the club with enthusiasm and efficiency but no one ever defeated him in an argument. His word was law.

By now, Greg had realised who he was insulting. He swallowed hard and then fell silent. The dog, now that its anger was exhausted, disdainfully trotted away and went to sniff at Lee's ankles.

'I wouldn't have believed that you would flout our rules in such a deplorable fashion, Gregory,' Mr Cantrill told him coldly. 'You know very well that no member is allowed to practise on the track itself before the day of the meeting – yet here you are, riding at a foolhardy speed, risking not only your own life and limb but that of an innocent dog!'

'But that dog shouldn't –' Greg, having found his voice, tried to interrupt.

'Silence!' the secretary thundered. 'Don't add to your crimes by trying to make excuses. There *are* no excuses to be made in a situation of this nature. If you don't know what the punishment is for this crime, then you're about to learn what it is. You are banned from the club's next meeting. Not just from riding – from attending it as well. If you are so witless as to try to sneak in, as you sneaked in here this evening, then the ban will be extended for the rest of the season. Now, do you understand?'

Greg was too stunned to be able to reply. He

nodded because there was no alternative. His helmet on his head again, he turned away to examine the state of the Shearsmith Special following its slide down the incline.

Lee, believing that he had escaped the secretary's wrath, was about to offer Greg his sympathy when Mr Cantrill spoke again.

'The same penalty will apply to you, Lee Parnaby,' was the fierce judgement.

'But why, Mr Cantrill?' the victim asked. His sense of horror matched Greg's.

'For what the courts, I believe, would describe as aiding and abetting. You may not have been riding while I was watching but I don't doubt that was your intention. In any case, it was your duty to *prevent* Gregory here from breaking the rules, not to connive at wrong-doing.'

'But, Mr Cantrill – '

'There is *no* appeal against our sentence,' said the secretary, swiftly cutting off Lee's protest. 'If you aren't aware of the rules then go and read them. Now, be off, both of you – and try to show good sense in future.'

Until they were out of sight of the two men, the boys didn't speak. But Lee noticed that Greg's knuckles, as he gripped the handle-bars of the Special, were white.

'What rotten luck!' Greg exploded, when they were in sight of the boundary road where his father was to pick them up. 'To come here on the one night Cantrill was strolling about with a mate! That must have been his mate's dog, too, because Cantrill doesn't have a dog – doesn't even like 'em much because they have a habit of attacking motorcyclists. I heard him say so when he told a spectator off at a meeting. Tell you what, I wish my Dad had stayed with us – he wouldn't have let Cantrill ban us on the spot.'

Lee made no reply. He was thinking that if he'd stuck to his original plan for the evening, he wouldn't have been anywhere near the Autodrome. In a way, he was really being punished for not keeping his appointment in the gymnasium.

'Still, I found out one thing,' Greg continued. 'The special is a really fantastic bike. I reckon it'll beat anything on the track – anything.'

'Maybe,' said Lee. 'But that's no good if you're not allowed on the track in the first place, is it? I mean, in a club race.'

Greg glared at him – and then retaliated, 'Well, you won't be winning anything at the next meeting, either, will you? Still, that's normal for you.'

Five

Two weeks later, on the day of Skalbrooke SMC's next meeting, Lee Parnaby and his cousin Joanne were on their way to the Great Lingdale Show. Jo, whose idea it was, couldn't conceal her delight; and, gradually, as the bus drew nearer to the showground, Lee began to feel that he might manage to enjoy the outing, too.

Nonetheless, he couldn't help thinking about what might be happening that afternoon at the Autodrome. As usual, Darren had gone off to the meeting with the highest hopes of winning the Intermediates' races and so getting his revenge at last on Graham Relton. 'I'll give you a lap-by-lap description of how I became the champion,' Darren had promised. Lee had just raised his eyebrows, shrugged and made no audible comment. He was rather thankful that Darren had stopped breaking into peals of laughter whenever the subject of the ban on Lee's attendance at the meeting was mentioned.

Mrs Parnaby had tended to share Darren's attitude; she'd told Lee that he deserved his fate because he should have been at the gymnasium, especially after he'd abandoned his cousin for that reason. Uncle Ken was reasonably sympathetic but, unlike Mr Shearsmith, had not offered to contact the secretary in the hope of getting the ban lifted. Privately, Lee believed that if Darren had been the offender their uncle would have been frantic in his efforts to smooth things over with Mr Cantrill. Probably, however Uncle Ken had realised he had no hope of succeeding where Mr Shearsmith had failed, even though Lee's offence was hardly in the same category as Greg's.

'Missing one meeting will just make you all the keener to do well at the next one,' Uncle Ken had insisted with what Lee easily recognised as a fairly feeble attempt to boost his morale. 'When you hear how Darren's got on you'll be trying harder than ever to emulate him.'

Joanne had said nothing at the time but he had sensed her sympathy; and then, later, she had commented that he'd obviously been treated most unfairly. She had a low opinion of Greg, anyway, and thought it was typical of him not to try to take all the blame on himself and so persuade the officials to let Lee compete. Then, the following week during her visit to the Parnabys' for tea, she had come up with the idea of visiting the Great Lingdale

Show which would be taking place at the same time as the club's meeting. She'd pointed out that one of the highlights would be 'A breathtaking display of skill and daring by an internationally-famed team of motor-cycle riders from Germany' (well, that was how the official programme described the event); and, in addition, there would be 'A brilliant exhibition of high-speed cutting and balancing by Canadian axe-men'.

'Sounds all right, I suppose, but none of it will be as good as actually *riding* in the motocross,' was Lee's response as he handed back Joanne's advance programme.

'Oh, I know,' she agreed, 'but at least it'll take your mind off what you're missing, Lee. And I'll try not to be a bore while we're together.'

His mother, of course, thought it was a splendid suggestion; she, coming in at that moment, had caught sight of the programme. One glance at it was enough.

'This is your chance to make it up to Joanne,' she said crisply. 'It's where she wants to go. So you're both going – and I don't want to hear a word of complaint from you, Lee.'

So Lee had surrendered. There didn't seem much point in battling on against such odds. All the same, he knew that however good the show might be, he'd spend most of his time thinking about Darren's chances of a victory at last that afternoon. If his brother *did* somehow manage to get a first he'd be absolutely impossible to live with for ever more; and at school everybody would know . . .

'Come on, Lee, snap out of those miserable thoughts!' Joanne said gaily as she steered him into the showground. 'I don't know *exactly* what you're thinking but I can make a jolly good guess. Look, the sun is shining, we've got money to spend, there's not a soul to tell us what we've *got* to do, so let's enjoy ourselves. Let's have a really *great* time. Tell you what, I'll buy you an ice-cream to start things off.'

So, contentedly licking chocolate-flake cornets, they went to stare at pens of sheep and pens of prime, snuffling porkers; at cages of drowsy rabbits and striding, strident cockerels; and to applaud the clever, precisely controlled driving by waggoners in charge of pairs of high-stepping shire horses in a competition held in the main show ring.

The next entertainment was to be one of the highlights of the day: the demonstration of their extraordinary and inventive talents by the axe-wielders from Canada. In common with the vast majority of spectators, Lee and Joanne had seen nothing like it anywhere. The men, dressed in trousers and singlets that displayed ample biceps, stood on huge logs and energetically cut them in half *between their feet* – and, what's more, did the

70

cutting at the fastest speed possible because they were in competition with each other to be the first to finish and jump down from the bisected log. One false slash and it could have been a foot that was removed, not a chunk of wood. But every axeman emerged from that contest quite unscathed.

Then the men split up into pairs to form three teams – and this time it was very solid-looking blocks of wood – thicker than telegraph poles – that they attacked. Taking alternate swings at the timber, they were again aiming to cut it in two and complete the operation ahead of the other two teams. Chips of wood were flying in all directions as the commentator on the loud-speaker system urged the various axemen on.

'You just wouldn't believe *anybody* could swing an axe as fast – and accurately – as that if you hadn't seen it for yourself, would you?' Jo exclaimed. And Lee, who'd been thinking exactly the same, nodded.

The final feat that the men performed was easily the toughest as well as the most spectacular. Two substantial poles, each several metres high, were propped upright in the centre of the ring. An axeman advanced on each and rapidly cut into the trunk at about waist-height; then, when he'd made a satisfactory V-shaped incision he slipped a plank of wood into the aperture so that it projected outwards like the branch of a tree. Nimbly he then

71

leapt on to that branch and, using it as a scaffold, cut into the pole again in exactly the same way. Raining blows on the timber he carved himself another foothold – inserted a plank – and thus gradually ascended to the top of the pole! The first one to reach the summit was, of course, the winner.

The volley of cheering and the applause that rang round the arena when the axemen completed their performance was almost deafening.

'Wow, that really was something!' Lee said, still savouring the agility and strength of the artists with the axes. 'I'd no idea the show was going to be as good as this. What's next?'

'Come on,' said Joanne happily, seizing him by the hand. 'There's something I'd like you to see. Different from what you've just seen but ...'

Lee didn't protest, even though he felt he was almost being dragged towards a marquee that bore the rather depressing word 'Handicrafts' on a board by its entrance. He couldn't imagine what on earth would interest her among tea-cosies and embroidered cushions and patterns of dried flowers. In fact, she led him to a section that had been turned into a small picture gallery. Paintings of all descriptions and standards hung against the canvas walls.

'Well, what do you think?' inquired Joanne, standing well back but staring fixedly at one row in particular.

'Well, what?' Lee was asking puzzledly until he

spotted a picture of a motor-cycle being ridden on what was plainly a motocross circuit. 'Oh, I see – yes, that's not bad at all.'

He went up to peer at it. 'Hey, Jo! Do you see, that's my number – it's – it's my bike! It's a painting of me right in the middle of the action.'

'Well done, Lee,' responded Joanne softly, breathing out in relief that he'd identified himself so quickly. She watched him read the label that was stuck temporarily to the frame.

'But – but, Jo, it's *your* picture!' he cried in genuine amazement, swinging round to face her. 'I didn't know you could paint like this. And to do a motocross picture of me. I think that's fantastic. It looks dead accurate. How did you manage that? You've hardly ever seen me racing.'

'Well, I see enough of bikes, don't I, so I just drew one. And it wasn't any problem to fit you on the bike, if you, er, see what I mean.'

Lee was now looking at a small blue sticker on the corner of the frame. 'Hey!' he said excitedly. 'You've actually won a prize as well! They've given you second prize. Terrific!' He paused and then asked, 'Is that why you wanted come here? Because you'd won a prize, I mean?'

'Hardly,' she answered. 'They didn't judge them until this morning. So I could only hope for the best that they'd accepted it for showing.'

'I don't know how you managed to keep quiet

73

about it for so long, Jo. I mean, if it had been mine, I'd have rushed over here as soon as we arrived and then told *everybody* about it.'

Joanne shook her head. 'No, you wouldn't, Lee. You're not the boastful type at all,' she told him. 'You're really quite good at a lot of things but you never let on to anybody if you can help it. I know – I'm a good observer, you see.'

Lee turned away and appeared to be taking a great interest in a painting of a fishing vessel unloading its catch. 'Er, I think I feel really hungry,' he announced. 'Do you know what I fancy? Fish and chips. I smelt them as we came past that takeaway cabin – terrific.'

'O.K. I expect I could manage some, too. Seems ages since I had my breakfast. Look, I'll pay for them to celebrate – I get a whole £1 for second prize so we'll blow the lot on best quality Great Lingdale Show fish 'n' chips!'

'Thanks very much,' said Lee with genuine gratitude, 'but I think I should pay my share. I'm always getting free meals at your place and that's not fair, really. And Uncle Ken always seems to pile twice as much on my plate as he gives to Darren. I've tried to tell him not to but he won't listen.'

Jo, however, insisted that it was her day out; and so pay she did, for both of them. As they shuffled forward in the queue – for, in spite of the sunshine, everybody seemed to want to lunch off fish-and-

chips – Joanne was silent for a time. Then, much
to Lee's surprise, she asked him if he'd ever felt
resentful when Darren received favourable treat-
ment.

'How do you mean?' Lee asked. The question
baffled him.

'Well, when there are just the two of you involved
in something, it's Darren, isn't it, who gets first
choice? You know, at motocross: first bike, first to
get new equipment and spares, first in everything,
really.'

Lee answered slowly, 'I hadn't really thought
about it. But it's natural, I suppose, because he's
older. Anyway, most people treat us alike – people
that really know us, I mean, such as relatives.'

'No they don't,' said Joanne quickly. 'Dad, for
one, doesn't treat you the same. That's why he
always gives you extra helpings of food. He feels
guilty because he shows Darren favouritism in
everything else.'

'Oh, I just thought Uncle Ken felt I needed
building up or something. I didn't think he had a
personal motive like that – unless it was to use up
some of the canned goods his firm sells!'

'Well, you can joke about it if you like, Lee, but
I don't think it's fair.'

At that point they reached the head of the queue;
and after they'd been served their mouths were too
full of delicious cod to make conversation. Then,

75

as they wandered towards the main show ring again, an announcement was made over the loudspeaker that the motor-cycle display would begin within the next five minutes.

'That's good timing,' said Lee, gulping down a chip that nearly seared his throat. 'Let's go and get a good position to watch from. I want to see if these guys are as good as the top scramblers.'

Afterwards, he was forced to admit that, in their own way, the German riders were incomparable. They rode as a team, cutting across each other's path on long diagonals with split-second timing at high speeds; they soared from ramps over each other's heads; they tore through colossal paper hoops simultaneously while travelling in opposite directions; and they even played a furious game of hockey ('a bit like polo on wheels,' as the commentator described it) in which the highlight was the feat of a goalkeeper who dribbled his way through the entire opposition to plant the ball in the net at the other end of the pitch.

'And now,' boomed the commentator, 'comes the chance for instant stardom for any youngster who has been thrilled by the superb riding we've all been watching. While the riders take a well-earned break before giving us their spectacular finale we're going to have a little competition.'

As he paused two men were wheeling out into the centre of the arena two junior-size motor-cycles. All the metal-work had been painted in gleaming white. Several metres away two other men were measuring out distances from beneath the high point of a ramp and, at intervals, placing white tapes in straight lines on the turf.

'This is a competition,' the commentator resumed, 'in which the young rider can emulate the skills of our top riders. As you see, a ramp has been set up – but not *too* high! – for flying jumps on a bike. Any youngster under the age of fourteen is invited to have a go – and the one who makes the biggest leap will win a special prize.

'One thing I must say before you all rush forward to compete: every contestant *must* wear the helmet, the knee pads and the elbow pads that we are providing. We want heroes to step forward – but we don't want them to be damaged before they can claim the big prize!

'Right, then, young gentlemen – or even young *ladies*, come to that – who's going to be the first? Who's going to set the target everyone will have to beat?'

Joanne, eyes shining, turned to Lee. 'Well, *you're* going to have a go, aren't you? I mean, it's *made* for you.'

Lee hesitated. 'Oh, I don't know. It's a bit like – well – showing-off, isn't it, with a huge crowd like this?'

'Rubbish!' responded Joanne positively. 'If

77

you're doing something that comes quite naturally to you then it can't be – what do they call it? – oh yes, exhibitionism. Anyway, if you're not going to have a shot at winning, I am.'

'*You* are? But how can you? I mean, have you ever ridden a real motor-bike, Jo? It's not the easiest – '

'Of course I have, Lee! You don't think I *ignore* those two bikes at home, do you? They're available, so I ride 'em when I feel like it – and that's quite often. And now I feel like shooting off that ramp. After all, it's not very high, is it? I'd be pretty feeble if I couldn't manage that.'

A moment later, Lee, still somewhat non-plussed, was staring at her back as she advanced determinedly into the arena. She seemed to have been springing surprises on him all day. But the biggest of them was certainly the news that she had been riding the motocross bikes. Yet it was typical of her to react in such a positive way to something that caught her interest.

He followed her into the centre of the show ring.

The commentator, who was also in charge of the event, was delighted to welcome a girl as the first contestant – and he made a fuss of her. Joanne stood there quite imperturbably as he babbled on about her initiative and sense of adventure and, he was sure, her 'terrific skills as a dare-devil rider'! Lee, when he was briefly interviewed, made no reference

78

to the fact that he and Jo were cousins, as a result of probing questions from the commentator, he admitted that he took part in schoolboy scrambles and had to suffer the consequences. The man with the microphone tried to make out that Lee must be 'a champion *rough*-rider in the making'. He was thankful when, after much cajolery, a few more candidates emerged from the crowd around the arena.

'I think that it should be ladies first,' announced the commentator predictably. 'So Joanne here, our *leading* lady, indeed our *only* lady competitor, is going to be the one to set the target all the rest have to aim at. I'm absolutely positive it's going to be a terrific one. So, Jo – I'm sure that's what they call you at home!– when the starter drops his hand, off you go.'

Joanne, by now wearing helmet and protective pads, had already been allowed to familiarise herself with the bike by riding it round in circles while the commentator was chatting to other contestants. There had been a draw among the boys for places in the line-up and the one to follow Joanne was similarly warming up on the far side of the long wooden ramp. Lee was to be the last but one to ride.

Now, coming round in a great sweep and building up speed, Joanne lined up her approach to the ramp. She looked, thought Lee, as if she'd spent

her life on the seat of a motor-cycle. No one would fault her style.

Up the ramp she roared, and through the air she soared, to touch down neatly and unwaveringly beyond the third tape. The crowd gave her a great cheer.

'What a fantastic performance by the little lady, Miss Joanne Wragby!' the commentator crowed ecstatically. 'That will really take some beating, folks. As I forecast, she could be a great winner: the *first* to have a go and the *first* at the finish.'

He'd forecast nothing of the kind but no one attempted to correct him. Everyone was watching the second rider zoom up the ramp. But he landed well short of Joanne's mark which was being indicated by a miniature yellow flag. The applause from the spectators, though, was still generous.

Lee, as he watched the others attempting to improve on Joanne's record, became increasingly nervous. He had a terrible fear that he was going to make a hash of his riding, that he would miss the ramp altogether or slide off it, sideways. He began to wish that he could get out of the arena without riding at all.

'O.K., son, your turn,' called one of the commentator's assistants to Lee. 'Time to get mounted.'

As he pulled on the helmet and the knee and elbow pads Lee suddenly recognised the man as one of the star performers in the German display team. He hadn't realised that they would bother to help out in what was really a children's sideshow.

'Not nervous, are you, son?' the man suddenly asked him. Lee, licking his lips, didn't know how to answer. 'No need to be, son. All you've got to do is enjoy yourself on this bike. Be confident! If you're confident in yourself, then you can do anything you want to do. O.K.?'

'O.K.,' replied Lee with a grin that was the result of a lot of effort.

'That's it, then! You look good on that bike – look as though you know what it's all about. Ridden before, have you?'

'Oh yes.'

'Thought so. You can always tell the tigers from the rabbits in this game. Right, away you go!'

Lee pulled away and began his sweep towards the starter. All at once, he felt at one with the bike. Next instant, he saw the starter's hand drop – and he raced towards the ramp.

Even as he took off, and experienced the thrill again of being airborne, he knew that his control of the bike was perfect; that his weight was in exactly the right place.

The touchdown, as far as he could tell, was also faultless and he felt a glow of triumph as the crowd roared its approval. As he wheeled away to return the bike to the organisers he saw that a yellow flag

was being planted a fraction ahead of the one marking Joanne's effort – and Joanne had still been in the lead when he made his jump.

'There you are, son, I told you everything would be great for you,' said the German rider as Lee handed over the bike. 'You see, all top people are a little nervous before they have to perform a special feat. That is a very good thing because it makes the adrenalin flow through the veins – and, zoom!, you give a better performance.'

'That was great!' Joanne enthused, giving him a hug. 'You've won, I reckon, because that lad riding now looks as though he might not even reach the top of the ramp!'

He did – but at such a speed that he had no chance at all of jumping beyond the first tape. The commentator himself led the applause for what he described as 'a brave try' and then announced the result of the competition:

'As you saw, ladies and gentlemen, two of the contestants finished well ahead of all the others. What's more, they finished so close together that we couldn't separate 'em! So the result is a dead heat – a dead heat between that plucky young lady, our very first rider, Miss Joanne Wragby, and the boy who would surely have won outright if it had been judged on style alone, Lee Parnaby. So, ladies and gentlemen, please give our super winners a big hand!'

Then, to their intense delight, he presented them with trophies: beautiful silver-plated models of the bikes they'd been riding. They were easily the best prizes Lee had ever seen.

'You know,' said Jo as they walked out of the arena together, 'I think they were a bit generous to me. You *should* have won outright, Lee. Still, I'm sure you will do at the next motocross after the way you rode today.'

Six

On the morning of the next meeting of the Skal-brooke Schoolboy Motorcycle Club it was Darren who was nearest to the telephone when it rang at his home. Because he was avidly reading a new motor-cycling magazine he didn't react for some moments; in any case, he was hoping that someone else would come along and answer it. Eventually, the caller's persistence broke down his resistance.

'Oh, hi, Joanne,' he said quite brightly when he recognised the voice. 'How are things with you?'

'Not so bad, Daz, but they're not going to be so good with you when you hear the news,' she told him briskly. 'Dad's not going to be able to take you and Lee and the bikes to the motocross today. He's had to – '

'What!' Darren screeched. 'He's got to! I'm all set for a great ride today, for a big win – I know it. He can't let us down like this, Joanne.'

'He didn't have any alternative. One of his salesmen has got into some sort of trouble and Dad had to go up to Newcastle last night to sort things out. Dad's the only one who could do it. There's no chance he'll be back home before Tuesday night, he told Mum. So – '

'O.K., so what about Aunt Sue? *She* can take us instead. She won't be much good at fixing the bikes but she can still drive us there – that's the main thing.'

'Sorry, no chance of that, either. You see, Dad – '

'*Somebody's* got to get us there!' Darren exploded. 'I just *can't* miss this meeting after having such rotten luck last time when that crazy idiot Nicholson knocked me off the bike. I *must* race today!'

'I expect Lee feels the same,' Joanne retorted coolly. 'Look, Daz, I think I'd better talk to him so that we can sort things out. He'll come up with some *useful* ideas.'

It seemed at first as if Darren were going to protest; but, perhaps thinking better of it, he put the phone down and went to yell for his brother. It didn't take him long to find him; Lee was helping to prepare a picnic lunch for all of them.

'It's a disaster!' Darren declared. 'Uncle Ken's let us down. So see what you can come up with, Lee.'

There were no futile interruptions from Lee as

87

Joanne explained that her father had been obliged to use the van to get to Newcastle because his company car was unluckily off the road for a few days; thus there was no vehicle that her mother could use.

'Dad did everything he could to get somebody else to take you and the bikes. He rang dozens of people, but no luck at all. They were all pretty sympathetic but just couldn't help. So it's pretty hopeless, Lee, unless *you* know somebody with the right sort of transport – and somebody who'd be willing to turn out on a Sunday. I know how much you've been looking forward to competing again – and Dad said to tell you how sorry he felt.'

As she talked Lee's mind was racing round all the names he could think of: people who might assist in a crisis. Unfortunately, his total didn't rise above four and each of them he had to discount for one reason or another.

Daz was tugging at his sleeve, desperate to know what was being decided.

'Come on, wonder brother,' he was saying between clenched teeth. 'You're supposed to be a genius at sorting out big problems.'

'Shut up a minute, Daz,' Lee told him. 'This isn't as simple as collecting your lost property off the chapel roof.'

To Lee's surprise, that did silence him. With Joanne, he resumed a discussion of possibilities until it was agreed that every one was an impossibility. So few people possessed a trailer or a van. Except . . .

'Hey, Jo, I've just thought of somebody!' he said excitedly. 'He's not *exactly* a mate of mine but he's always very friendly and seems to like me. Got just the right transport for us, too. Big old grocery van – bags of room if he removes the shelves.'

'Who's that, then?'

'Oh, Mr Thirlwell. He's the travelling greengrocer that comes round here – has been doing for years. His van's almost *prehistoric* but he looks after it like a – like a family pet. He lives not so far from here so it would be easy to get to see him. I'll get off now.'

'Would it help, Lee, if I came as well? I mean, perhaps I could help in some way – or just help to persuade him. If you tell me where it is I'll meet you there – won't take long on my push-bike. Could be that two heads are better than one – that's what Mum always says.'

Lee agreed and explained how to get to Mr Thirlwell's. Then he rang off and told his anxious brother what he had in mind. Darren, predictably, didn't think much of the idea. It seemed that he hadn't a high opinion of the greengrocer, though he admitted he'd never actually talked to him.

'Have you a better suggestion?' Lee asked as he hurried to the door.

'Er, no.'

'Thought not,' Lee flung back over his shoulder.

He was in luck. Mr Thirlwell was at home, relaxing with a Sunday newspaper, following, as he put it, a hearty breakfast.

'Well, this is a pleasure, Lee – and a most unexpected one,' the greengrocer greeted him, beamingly. 'You've run out of vitamins, haven't you? That's what you've come for, isn't it?'

'Not, er, exactly, Mr Thirlwell. I want to borrow your van.'

To Lee's surprise, the greengrocer didn't even blink; and his smile didn't fade. 'Ah, is that it? Well, now, what use do you have in mind for it?'

'To transport motor-bikes – mine and my brother Darren's – to the motocross club meeting. It's today, you see, and Uncle Ken, who usually takes us, well, he – '

Before he could get any further the front door bell rang; and, guiltily, Lee guessed who it would be. Until that moment he'd forgotten he should have waited outside the house for Joanne to arrive. Mr Thirlwell peered through the bay window and remarked that it appeared to be his day for receiving young visitors.

Hastily, Lee explained, as Mr Thirlwell let her in, that Joanne was his cousin and that it was her father who normally attended to all their travel and riding arrangements. Patiently, the greengrocer listened to the entire story from the two of them without interrupting once.

'Fascinating!' he pronounced when they finished. 'I'd no idea that this scrambling business was so highly organised – or that all you youngsters were involved. I've always like motor-cycles because in my Army days I used to ride one, most of the time. I was in the Royal Signals and they're the real experts at that game – their motor-cycle displays at the big tournaments were always the highlight. Oh, yes!

'Still, I mustn't bore you with my reminiscing. Time mustn't be lost. So, let's get off to the garage and see to the van.'

Lee was quite stunned. 'You mean, you *will* help us?'

'Of course, young Lee! What are friends for but to help when the need arises?'

As they followed Mr Thirlwell to the garage at the bottom of a long, narrow garden Lee and Joanne exchanged delighted whispers.

'I never imagined it would be so *easy*.'

'Tell you what, Daz is going to get a shock when we turn up with the bikes surrounded by apples and oranges and spuds!'

In fact, somewhat to their disappointment, the ancient van was almost empty. Mr Thirlwell explained that, instead of making his rounds on a Monday, he went off to the wholesale market to replenish his supplies for the first half of the week. They helped him to remove various crates and sacks and some of the shelves; the one item they were asked to treat with great reverence was the pair of old-fashioned ('but wonderfully accurate – just as good as your new-fangled computer') brass weighing scales.

'There, I think that'll give you all the room you need for a couple of bikes,' Mr Thirlwell said. 'So hop in the front with me and give me directions to your home, Joanne. I must say, I'm quite looking forward to this race meeting of yours. It's going to seem quite like old times for me to be surrounded by motor-cycles – and to sniff that most distinctive of smells, the mixture of petrol and oil. Lovely!'

Almost as if the racing spirit had suddenly got into his blood, he drove the van at a rattling rate; yet he still found time to wave to favoured customers he spotted in their gardens or out walking. Some of them displayed astonishment at seeing him driving his van on a Sunday morning – and at such speed.

Aunt Sue took their arrival in a greengrocer's van in her stride and watched with interest as the racing bikes were propelled up a makeshift ramp and then secured for the journey to the Autodrome.

They were climbing back into the cab when Joanne's mother put her hand on Lee's shoulder as if to detain him.

'There isn't anything you've forgotten, is there, Lee?' she inquired.

Lee frowned and thought hard. Eventually, still puzzled, he had to admit that he couldn't think of anything they'd overlooked.

'How about,' asked his aunt with a grin, 'your . . . *brother?*'

'Oh, murder! Daz! I *had* forgotten him. But, you see, he didn't think we'd find any transport. So . . . Still, we'll just have to go and pick him up and – '

'No, don't worry, Lee,' Aunt Sue said quickly, still smiling. 'All's well. Darren has been on the phone to me – trust him! – to say he's making his own way to the Autodrome and that he'll meet you there – if, as he put it, you manage to find a jet-propelled horse-and-cart. I rather gathered that he was hoping to borrow a bike from somebody.'

'He would! I'll bet he didn't think of trying to borrow a bike for me. Typical of him to think only of himself. Still, he'll get a bit of a shock when we roll up with our own bikes in this terrific transporter!'

'Only,' pointed out the driver of the transporter in a surprisingly firm voice, 'if we get a move on *now.*'

Seven

In the paddock the greatest amount of attention was being paid to the Shearsmith Special. Relays of parents and fellow competitors kept coming up to admire the gleaming black machine but none of them could extract any of its technical secrets from Greg or his father, although they weren't denying that the bike's exhaust system was, as Mr Shearsmith put it, 'where it all happens.' One of the marshals who'd been to look at it had another view. 'Maybe it does all happen down there,' he muttered to a friend, 'but in the final analysis everything depends on the skills of the rider – and young Greg'll need to learn how to control himself during a race before he gets the best out of that bike. And after being suspended I reckon he'll be riding in a crazier fashion than ever.'

Greg's confidence – already as high as the clouds on a gloriously sunny day – had received a boost when he learned that, for this meeting,

94

they'd be going round the circuit in the opposite direction.

'That's bound to give you and me a big advantage,' he chortled to Lee when they met a few minutes after the arrival of Mr Thirlwell's van. 'All the other riders will have to adjust to the new course after the last meeting. But as we didn't race then we won't have to think about what happened last time. We'll make a flying start while they're still working out which way to go!'

Lee wasn't at all convinced by that argument but he didn't say so. He wasn't going to do anything to jeopardize the offer of help he and Darren had received from Greg's father.

Mr Shearsmith had come across to them as soon as they'd begun to unload the bikes in the car park. Initially, he wanted to say how much appreciation he had for Lee's loyalty at the time of the suspension because, he said, it would have been so easy for Lee to protest that Greg had led him astray; instead, Lee, in Mr Shearsmith's words, had 'acted and taken your punishment like a man – without a whimper.' Now, when he discovered that the brothers' uncle was unable to be present, he had volunteered his services as mechanic and general assistant. The offer was accepted with alacrity by Lee; they needed somebody to tune and, if necessary, service their bikes because he'd already discovered that, helpful though Mr Thirlwell wanted to be, his knowledge of modern motocross machines was virtually nil.

'I'll keep you in top racing condition,' Mr Shearsmith promised, 'even if it means that you beat Greg to the chequered flag in the process!'

Darren, when he arrived a few minutes later, actually managed to sound grateful for once for the arrangements Lee had made on his behalf. He'd caught a bus from home into town. Then he was lucky enough to get a lift to the Autodrome from the parents of a club member who'd been filling up with petrol at a self-service station near the bus stop. Darren admitted that he'd been worrying about who would attend to their bikes in Uncle Ken's absence if his brother did succeed in getting them delivered to the track.

'But I didn't think you'd do it,' he told Lee; and then added in typical fashion, 'I assumed it was going to be another desperately unlucky day for me – for us, I mean.'

Joanne and Lee exchanged a laugh about that remark as soon as they were out of earshot. While Darren remained in the paddock to discuss tactics and performances with his cronies, his brother and cousin decided to walk the circuit and watch the cadets, the youngest riders, in action in the first scramble of the day. Inevitably, they found themselves rivetted by events at V-One, the most acute of the severe bends on the oval-shaped course. Far too many of the riders seemed unable to judge the speed at which they could hope to negotiate it – and so bikes and bodies were catapulting in several directions.

'I just hope you're not going to go the same way!' Joanne said to Lee as she helped to lift one tiny boy to his feet and then reunited him with his bike. Although the rider was seven years old he looked much younger.

'Don't worry, I've worked out just what's right for this corner,' Lee assured her. 'I doubt, though, that Greg has. In these fast conditions I reckon there'll be an almighty pile-up here if Greg gets himself in the leading group – and I don't see where else *he* will be!'

'This dip into the bend is going to make it even more difficult. It'd be mad to come down into this at anything more than – what? – third gear?'

He grinned. 'One thing's definite – if you arrive here flat out, that's where you'll finish: flat out on your back on a stretcher. Have you noticed how many St John ambulancemen are stationed here?'

It was also the place for overhearing hard-luck stories related by other spectators. The most amazing one concerned the rider whose bike simply snapped in two, with the rear half flying across the track and knocking another competitor from his machine. Joanne shuddered when she heard that one.

Silently and thoughtfully, Joanne and Lee made their way back towards the paddock while the cadets were on their final circuit. The Juniors would be racing before Lee went out to ride but he wanted to check over his bike again and perhaps have a word with Mr Shearsmith. But they paused as one rider swerved recklessly across the track and very nearly charged through the marker tapes alongside them.

At least one spectator was quite unmoved by that dangerous manœuvre. At that moment he was telling his companion earnestly, 'You know, my Dad will brain me if I don't get a high place today. He says if I don't start improving rapidly everyone will know he's got an *idiot* for a son!'

Joanne's eyebrows shot up. Then she whispered to Lee: 'Well, at least you don't have *that* sort of pressure to put up with, do you?'

'No,' Lee agreed, 'but I do have a mad brother to cope with! And you never know what he's going to do next. He'll be desperate to win today to get even with Graham Relton. He really does hate Graham and I don't think he could stand another failure if Graham wins.'

'But he's not going to win, is he, Lee? It's *your* turn today for the chequered flag.'

'Oh, come on, Jo,' Lee replied lightly, 'I'll need a heck of a lot of luck to overtake Gray Relton if he's really in top form. He's easily the best in

98

our age group and he's got a great machine. So I reckon – '

He stopped as, without warning, Joanne dashed away. For a moment, he thought he'd said something to offend her, though he couldn't imagine what it was. Then he saw that she was making for one of the market stalls where people were selling riders' clothing and equipment and even such oddities as woolly toys (presumably to tempt parents with young children complaining that they were being neglected).

Before Lee could reach her Joanne had made a purchase and was coming back towards him.

'There you are!' she said triumphantly. 'That should bring you all the luck you need. The rest of the race depends on your determination, Lee. I think you've got all the skill you need.'

She handed him a key-ring with the glossy black leather tab cleverly cut into the shape of a cat.

'Thanks, Jo,' was all he could think of saying. Then, noting the expression on her face, he added, 'I'll carry it with me always. And I'll put every key I get on it.'

He was still fingering the key-ring in his trouser pocket when they returned to the paddock. Practically the first person he saw was Darren, strutting almost possessively between the rows of bikes in company with one of his cronies. It was obvious that Daz had found someone to attend to his own

99

machine. By now, Lee surmised, his brother would have convinced himself that it was his own idea to travel to the meeting in Mr Thirlwell's spectacular van. Certainly Daz appeared to be in a confident mood.

'It's in beautiful condition, isn't it?' Lee remarked as he trailed his fingers lightly over the frame of his green-and-silver motor-cycle. He'd already had a practice ride round the circuit but he was wishing that he could go out again before the race started.

'Well, it should be, considering all the hours that Dad spends on it every week,' Jo was saying. 'He wouldn't devote any more time to it if it were my bike, I reckon. One of these days someone is going to show him that girls can tackle motocross just as well as boys ...'

Lee wasn't really listening to her. The announcement was being made that the riders in the Intermediates' race should move towards the starting gate. The butterflies in his stomach fluttered with the abandon of the pennants above the riders' helmets when the throttles opened up. He glanced across at his brother, who had drawn a place almost alongside the starter, but Darren was staring fixedly ahead. Like every other rider, he knew that a flying start was essential.

One of the spectators was suddenly calling attention to the plight of a boy whose engine had cut out. The bike was wheeled out of the line and frantic efforts were made by the lad's father to restore power. Anxiously, other riders fiddled with helmet straps or goggles or just prayed that the starter would get on with his job. Every second of waiting was an extra burden on the nervous system. For many of the contestants, it wasn't only the warmth of the day that was causing them to sweat so freely.

The starter's knuckles whitened – and, next instant, the tape concertinaed across the track.

The scramble was on!

As the field spurted away, Lee felt a sharp blow on his right leg which very nearly caused him to collide with the bike on his left. He had been struck into by the rider of a very battered-looking Yamaha who seemed unable to control his machine. Lee couldn't identify the boy under his dusty helmet.

Already he had lost ground as a result of his instinctive swerve away from the Yamaha. But as soon as he engaged a higher gear he sensed that his bike was in top racing condition. Just what Mr Shearsmith had done to it he had no idea; but the engine note was a perfect melody.

By the first S-bend, Graham Relton had established a useful lead with the bounding Greg Shearsmith in second place. Lee, breaking away from the tail-enders, was able to see that Darren was not among the leading group as, briefly, the pace-setters came back towards him. Then they hurtled away again in the direction of the first of the major hazards: V-Two.

As the riders went into the next, and well-banked, bend, marshals were already shouting warnings to cut down on speed. The race was being run at an electrifying rate with Greg snapping at Graham's rear wheel. He was putting on all the power he possessed in order to overtake the leader. Yet they were not drawing far ahead of the pack behind them. In these fast conditions everyone seemed to believe he could set up a personal lap record.

Lee, now weaving his way through to the middle of the field, edged forward on his bike as he approached V-Two. For such a severe bend the rider's balance had to be absolutely correct.

Then, just as he decided on his line of navigation, a Suzuki slithered perilously right across his path from the left. Lee hadn't even been aware that the rider was so close to him; but the boy had lost control in the ultra-fast racing conditions while in too high a gear.

Deftly, Lee changed down again even as he steered sharply to his left, and then regained his chosen course with another flick of his wrists. Now he had enough momentum to carry him round the corner at what had to be maximum speed for the day. As he completed the switch-back he saw that the Suzuki rider was being helped to his feet by ambulance attendants.

That near-scrape, and the way he had avoided trouble, set the adrenalin flowing again and also gave a great boost to his confidence. He began to believe that this could be his day after all. Moments later he was blasting superbly over a jump and landing with immense style; so much so that he won a spontaneous round of applause from hardened spectators more used to cheering on only their own sons and daughters.

With only half a lap completed he had overtaken half-a-dozen riders and was now among the main pack – and no more than a couple of lengths adrift of his brother. As usual, Darren's black-and-yellow striped helmet was easily picked out; but, for some reason, the self-styled 'Tiger of the Track' was not competing with his customary snarling endeavour. He had allowed the cut-throat leaders, Gray Relton and Greg Shearsmith, to pounce into a clear lead. Those two were having a battle all to themselves as they scorched into V-One, the toughest test on the entire track.

They went into it side by side, neither willing to concede so much as a centimetre in room or deviate a fraction off the chosen route to success. Inevitably, they touched – and it was Greg's glossy black machine that went careering off course. Graham, slim and slightly built and fragile in appearance, was really as strong as whipcord; in a physical contest, he'd rarely come off second best. He wasn't going to now, either.

Greg, trying desperately to correct his deflection, overdid it. Unwilling to lose even a single rev, he tried to keep up with his rival – and paid the predictable penalty. He was catapulted from the jackknifing Special and soared over the perimeter tape to land in a heap among the scattering spectators.

Graham, displaying no emotion at all behind his dust-free goggles, roared on into a clear lead. At that moment, he had every reason to assume that he was on course for another triumph.

With the help of by-standers and an alarmed ambulanceman, Greg was quickly on his feet and assuring everyone that he was still in good shape and determined to get back into the race. His father had sprinted across to scrutinize the Special and ensure that it had suffered no major damage. Then, with a command to Greg to 'Stick to it!' Mr Shearsmith pushed him back on to the bike and into the race. Before the nearest marshal could blink a second time, Greg was speeding away.

Nonetheless, he had lost more than a share of the lead. Several of the riders who had been trying to break away from the pack behind Relton and Shearsmith at last succeeded after rounding V-One. Darren Parnaby, inspired by the sight of Greg's dramatic departure from the track, made

the most positive charge. After his earlier worries, he was beginning to get over the absence of Uncle Ken, who had always given him so much encouragement. Daz was no longer looking out for him and his signals at crucial stages of a race. This time he was on his own and would have to ride his own race. On the brief straight he engaged top gear – and in an instant he seemed to be flying.

Lee, too, judged that it was time to increase his own pace. V-One proved to be a less daunting obstacle than he'd supposed. He sensed now that he was riding near the top of his form – and the sight of Darren's helmet, bobbing just ahead of him, was an additional spur. But he wanted to pick precisely the right moment to sweep past his brother.

So, after sniping his way through the field, Lee was lying in fifth position at the end of the first of the four laps. Graham Relton possessed such a substantial lead that some spectators were talking about the only race being the one for second place.

One man, though, who hadn't written off his son's chances of victory was Harry Shearsmith. Darting across the oval, from vantage point to vantage point, he was urging Greg to greater efforts – and Greg, being Greg, was responding as best he could. Before another circuit had been completed he was again among the challengers – and by now Darren was in second place, only just in front of his younger brother. Lee felt that he could 'take' Daz whenever he wanted to but he was biding his time. His machine was responding beautifully to every demand he made of it ... and he knew that he had plenty of power in reserve.

'Just look at that kid on the black bike!' one spectator was yelling to another. 'He's really the wild one. If only he'd settle down he could be a world-beater. He's been on the floor once and now he's battling for second place again – but look at the way he's riding. He's all over the place!'

Greg had realised only a split-second before the man spoke that something was wrong with his steering. But the fault, he was certain, would rapidly correct itself – nothing went wrong with a bike his father serviced. Having carved his way back into a springboard position, Greg wasn't going to drop back for any reason.

At that moment, Lee decided to deliver the telling thrust and accelerate past Darren. All three riders were in one of the narrowest sections of the track, with shallow banking on both sides of the slight downhill gradient. Lee wanted his brother to *know* exactly who had relegated him to third place.

Lee aimed to burst past on Darren's left. With a right-hander coming up, Daz wouldn't expect to be challenged on that side. So the element of surprise would also be in Lee's favour.

He moved out – and then surged forward. Momentarily, the bikes were level. Daz, glancing sideways, was startled to see that it was his brother. Briefly, his control wavered; the bikes came together, the boys' knees touched. Then, instinctively, Daz steered to the right. In the moment that they parted Greg pounced with the intention of driving through the gap between them.

It was then that the steering on the Shearsmith Special let him down. The erratic course he'd been following had actually been forced on him by the looseness of the handlebars, damaged when he crashed. In his eagerness to get Greg back into the race Harry Shearsmith had failed to spot the defect.

Greg, unable to manœuvre his machine, banged

fiercely into the rival on his right. Darren was flung into the banking; and from there he slid in a sitting position to the ground, an expression of astonishment rather than pain visible beneath his goggles. The Special wobbled precariously back and forth across the track for several lengths before it, too, collapsed.

By then, Lee, miraculously unaffected by the earlier touch from Daz's bike, was clear of all trouble. In one fell swoop two of his deadliest rivals were out of the race. Now he was in second place with his nearest pursuer almost fifty metres behind him.

'Go *on*, Lee, you can do it!' someone yelled to him – and one glance at the slim figure beside the track told him that it was Joanne. She had seen that there was nothing for him to worry about now as long as he had the speed to catch Graham Relton.

Lee was optimistic. He knew that his luck was in, just as Darren's was out. For once, his brother's inevitable claim that he'd been the victim of bad luck would be justified. Lee thought of the black cat key-ring in his pocket – and powered on.

His style on the straights, as he positioned himself on the bike to keep the front wheel skipping over the bumps at maximum speed, drew cheers from the spectators. Metre by metre he closed the gap between himself and the leader.

Graham, suddenly made aware by the screeching of his fans that he had a challenger, risked a backward glance just as he approached V-One for the last time. As his concentration momentarily faltered, so did his control of the bike. The wobble was enough for him to lose his momentum.

Exultantly, Lee seized his chance to storm into the lead on the final, crucial corner in a flurry of dust.

As the flag fell and he zipped across the finishing line, two lengths ahead of Graham Relton, his arms went up in sheer delight.

'That was wonderful, Lee, really wonderful,' Joanne greeted him as he swept into the paddock.

'I just wish Dad had been here to see you win your first motocross.'

'I didn't need him, Jo. It was you who brought me luck – you and your black cat.'

'Rubbish!' she said, trying not to blush. 'You didn't need luck. You won because you were good enough to win and because you *wanted* to win. Most of all, because you believed you could win. That counts more than luck.'

Lee grinned. 'If you say so,' he told her.

The story of Lee Parnaby's adventures continue in *Fast From The Gate* and *Tiger of the Track*, published by Magnet Books.